803 WISHING LANE

A CHERRY FALLS ROMANCE

SHAW HART

Copyright © 2021 by Shaw Hart

contact@shawhart.com

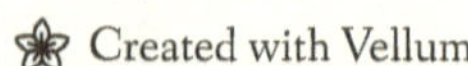 Created with Vellum

*

How did one camping trip go this wrong?

Caroline Park moved to Cherry Falls to raise her niece. It was supposed to be a fresh start, a clean slate for both of them. She bought the Virgin Street Diner and thought that she could lose herself in work and learning how to be a single parent.

When she finally gives in to Charlotte's plea to go camping one weekend, it's just supposed to be a one night trip, but when it starts to pour and Caroline can't see the road anymore, they're forced to stop at the nearest house for help.

Too bad for Caroline that house belongs to Heath Winters.

Heath Winters is gruff and a bit of a loner. He's also a thorn in Caroline's side and has been ever since she moved to town. Unfortunately for her, there's no other option.

Heath has wanted Caroline since he first saw her, but his lack of social skills seem to have done nothing but push her away.

Will one rainy night in his cabin be enough time for Heath to turn things around and convince his girls that they belong with him?

ONE

Caroline

"DON'T FORGET YOUR BACKPACK, BUNNY," I remind Charlotte, my niece, as she climbs out of her car seat.

She smiles up at me, grabbing my hand as I help her out of the back seat. It's then that I notice a stray smear of yogurt on her upper lip and I grab a baby wipe from the backseat, wiping it away before I take her hand and lead her up to the preschool.

I've been Charlotte's legal guardian since she was just over three years old. My brother, Calvin, and his wife, Shelby, were killed in a car accident. They were headed for a short vacation, just an overnight stay, and were killed. It had been the first time they left Charlotte and I had promised to take care of her. I guess I should have been more worried about them.

My brother and I were always super tight. I was his best man at his wedding and the godmother of his kid. He supported me through college and I even moved back to New York and lived near him and Shelby, with my best friends, Sayler and Coraline.

Our parents had both died when I was young and it was just me and Calvin, so when he passed, I was the only option left for Charlotte. My brother was a few years older than me, and he had been the one to care for me when they died. It's been a few years and I still don't think I've got a handle on this whole parenting thing.

The first few months that I was her legal guardian were rough. We both cried all of the time. It was hard to explain to her what happened and why her mom and dad weren't coming back. I took her to three different therapists before we found one that seemed to help her, and we did family therapy together, too. I was willing to do anything to help her but she was too young to really grasp the idea that her parents couldn't come back.

The therapist told me that it would be better for me to wait until she was old enough to understand the concept of death before I brought it up to her again. Until then, I'm her mom.

"We're painting today, Aunt Caro," Charlotte tells me as she takes my hand and skips alongside me to the front door.

"What are you going to paint?" I ask her, holding the door open and leading her down the hallway to her classroom.

"Our family! And a castle. Oh! Or maybe a tent. It will be us this weekend when we go camping!" she says excitedly.

I smile down at her, loving her enthusiasm. Her teacher, Ms. Newton, smiles when Charlotte hops into the room, hanging her backpack up and running over to her friends who are already seated on the alphabet rug in the corner.

"Bye, bunny!" I call after her, waving at Ms. Newton before I hurry back out to my car.

Charlotte and I moved to Cherry Falls a few months ago after I bought the town diner. We both needed a change of pace and when I came by to see the Virgin Street Diner, I fell in love with the small town.

Charlotte loves it here, too, and that was the big selling point. I even took her house shopping and she picked out an old Victorian house that was painted a pale pink. There was a white picket fence and some chicken coops in the backyard.

That was another big selling point. Charlotte is obsessed with animals. She wants to adopt every single one that she sees and if she had it her way, we would own a dozen dogs and cats, chickens, geese, a random mean goat, some pigs, and about a hundred bunnies. I'm sure it's easy to tell which animal is her favorite.

In the end, we just adopted two dogs. We went for one, but they were bonded and I just couldn't separate them. I try to tell myself that it teaches Charlotte responsibility since she has to help me feed and walk them.

My phone starts to ring as I drive across town to the diner and I smile when I see Sayler's name on my phone screen.

"Hey!" I answer with a smile.

"Hey, boo! Are you busy?" she asks and I can hear some dishes clinking in the background.

She must be at home with her boyfriend Rooney. I met him when he came to visit with her last month and he seems like a really good guy. He makes Sayler happy and that's all that matters to me.

"I'm never too busy for you. How are things going?"

"Great! Rooney and I were thinking about taking a trip and renting a cabin somewhere next month. Since I know you could always use a break and Charlotte is obsessed with camping, I thought I would see if you wanted to join us."

"Oh, I'd love to join you on your couple vacation," I tease and she laughs.

"It's not like that! I think Harvey is going to join us and maybe Gray and Nora," she says, naming two other guys who work at Eye Candy Ink with Rooney.

"Where are you going and when?" I ask, pulling into the parking lot of the diner.

"We don't know yet. We're pretty flexible and I know with Charlotte you have more to coordinate, so if you want to come, we can work around you."

"Can I think about it and get back to you tonight? I need to check our schedules."

"Of course! I'll talk to you later, Caro!"

"Bye, Say," I say with a laugh.

I park in my spot next to the back door of the Virgin Street Diner and hurry inside. My employees, Ezra and David, are already inside, helping the early bird customers. Amelia, my last employee scheduled to come in, should be in just in time for the lunch rush.

"Morning, David!" I call as I head past where he's busy cooking.

"Morning," he grunts back at me, his familiar beanie on his head.

David is a bigger guy with a big beard. He should look out of place at the '50s style diner, but somehow he fits right in. He worked here for the old owner and I was lucky enough to convince him to stay and work for me.

I hang my things up in the back office, tying my black

hair up in a high ponytail before I head out to the floor.

"Hey, Ezra," I greet the young waiter.

"Hey, Ms. Park."

Ezra dips into the kitchen to grab some more napkins for a table and I head over to the coffee pot and start making another pot since we're low.

The Virgin Street Diner is already busy and I get to work, refilling drinks and taking the orders of anyone who sits at the counter. I make sure that the coffee pots never run out and check everyone out.

The Virgin Street Diner is a retro kind of diner with a red and white checkered floor and a jukebox on the back wall. There's even an old-school cash register up front next to the dessert display.

Things start to take a lull around 10 am and I help Ezra refill the salt and pepper bottles on all of the tables and booths. Amelia comes in at 11:30 and things start to pick up again.

The Virgin Street Diner is one of the more popular places in Cherry Falls and we usually stay busy throughout the day. We're in the middle of the afternoon lull when *he* walks in.

Heath Winters.

He comes in everyday around 2 pm and sits at the counter. Ezra is getting ready to leave for the day and Amelia is in the back, refilling the ketchup and mustard bottles, so it's just me and him out front.

"Your usual?" I ask as Heath sits down.

He always orders the same thing. The Holy Roller Burger, medium well, with French fries, a glass of water, and a slice of cherry pie.

"Yeah," he grunts, settling onto the stool at the counter. "How's your day going, Caroline?"

He asks me this every day. Unfortunately, things usually spiral downward from there. I finish writing out his order on my pad and add it to the queue.

"Good. How about you?"

"Can't complain," he says, taking a sip of his water as I set it down in front of him.

Heath is a bit of a loner. He's gruff and can be short with people. He and I got off on the wrong foot when I first got to town and we've never seemed to come back from it. I know that he tries to be civil, but it always seems to rub me the wrong way.

"Got any plans for this weekend?" Heath asks as I grab him his slice of pie.

"I'm taking Charlotte to Wild Ridge Mountain. She's been dying to go camping, so we're headed up there for the night."

"Sounds like fun. Have you ever been camping before?" he asks.

"Um, no, but how hard can it be, right?"

"You should stop by the Trading Post. I can give you a discount on some of the gear and show you how to use it."

His offer has me taken aback and feeling a little antsy. Normally this is about the time he says something to piss me off, such as he likes my hair better up because I don't look so overheated, or that I should take a break and get off of my feet more.

I know it's just me. Heath isn't the type to be purposefully mean. It's just that I was asked so many questions about if I could really handle caring for Charlotte before I was allowed to be her legal guardian, and now any hint of someone doubting my abilities has me feeling on edge.

I know what I'm capable of and I hate when people doubt me.

Plus, who tells a woman that she looks overheated? Alright, maybe it is a little bit Heath.

"Uh, thanks. Maybe I'll take you up on that."

His order comes up and I pass it across the counter to him, sliding his bill after.

"I'm headed to get Charlotte now but Amelia will help you if you need anything else."

"Thanks, Caroline," he says softly and for just a moment, my walls start to crumble.

I'd be lying if I said that I wasn't attracted to Heath. He's a good-looking guy. Tall with a stable job and a full head of thick brown hair. That's practically a unicorn to a woman in her thirties.

I've been fighting my feelings toward him, though, because I don't want to upset Charlotte. We're still getting settled here and I don't want to throw that off. Hell, I'm still figuring out how to be a parent and balance mom life and work life. Besides, I don't want Charlotte to feel like she isn't the most important person to me. I never want her to doubt how much she is loved.

Still, I can't stop myself from taking one last look over my shoulder at Heath as I head to grab my purse.

He's looking at me, those deep green eyes of his trained on my blue ones and I freeze, trapped in his gaze. There's something in the way that he's looking at me, but I can't quite decipher it.

"Excuse me, Caroline," Amelia says, breaking the staring contest that I was having with Heath.

I step aside, letting her carry out the tray of ketchup bottles before I head for the office and then out to my car.

As I back out of my spot, I know one thing for sure.

I can't go to his shop for the camping gear. If I do, I just might lose my heart.

TWO

Heath

I WATCH as Caroline turns and heads back into the kitchen, my heart thumping loudly as she disappears from my sight. It's always like that when I see her. It has been since the first time I laid eyes on her.

I can still remember the first time I came into the Virgin Street Diner after Caroline had bought it. I had taken one look at her and fallen head over heels in love with her. I've never been very good with women but I really messed up with my sweet Caroline.

When I had first come in, I sat at the counter, hoping to work up the nerve to ask her out. Then the little girl coloring at the other end of the counter had run over and hugged her and the family resemblance was so strong that I knew they were related. I assumed that she was her daughter and that my girl was taken and just like that, all my dreams of being with this girl were dashed.

When she took my order, I might have been a little short

with her. I was frustrated that someone beat me to her and I took that out on her. She had tried to be nice to me, but I shut her down, giving her the cold shoulder. I've been paying for it ever since.

Caroline isn't taken. I should have looked for a ring before I opened my mouth. I've been working on getting back in her good graces ever since that first day.

So far, I've failed.

Miserably.

I thought that I could be patient but I might have overestimated the limits of my patience. I keep trying to talk to her but she hasn't opened up to me much; I can't really say that I blame her.

My best friend, Jacob Sten, says that I need to just suck it up and ask her out already. He says that's how he got his wife, Amelia. I'm beginning to think that maybe he's right. I need to just man up and tell her how I feel. I'm only torturing myself by prolonging it and longing for her.

I pay my bill, nodding goodbye to Amelia as I head out the door, and head back toward my shop which is right across the street from the Virgin Street Diner. I pass by Dr. Coleman in the parking lot and stop to say hi to him. He's just getting out of his car and he looks frazzled.

"Hey, doc. How's it going?" I ask.

He sighs, dragging a hand through his hair. "Busy. I was just stopping in to grab a bite to eat before I head back to the office."

"No luck finding a new nurse yet?" I guess and he nods.

"I put a new ad up for one. Hopefully I can find someone soon."

"Good luck," I say, waving as he hurries into the diner and I make my way back to the trading post.

I unlock the doors and head inside, flipping the lights

back on. I've owned the Trading Post for close to a decade now. I bought it right after I moved to town. The old owner was ready to retire and I had jumped at the chance to buy it.

Cherry Falls is a typical small town. Everyone knows everyone else and all of their business. The crime rate is next to zero and there's never any traffic. Besides, it's beautiful here with the mountains on one side and water on the other.

Small towns have always suited me more than big cities. I don't really like crowds, and I tend to do better talking to people one-on-one. Most people would call me gruff. They'd be right but the real truth is that I just never know what to say to people, especially people that I don't know.

Some people are born with the gift of gab but I was never one of those people.

My parents were, though. My mom and dad were both born and raised in a small town just like Cherry Falls. We lived up in the mountains in this little tourist spot and they owned a gift shop and a small ice cream parlor right on Main Street. They could make anyone who walked through the door feel like family. It was a gift, really.

Me, I liked working in the back where I could stick to myself. There have only been a handful of people that I feel comfortable around. Jacob and Caroline are the only ones that I've ever met where I felt at ease as soon as I saw them. Maybe that's why I'm so obsessed with Caroline.

I head to the back office, grabbing another box of sweaters that I need to stock and carry them out onto the floor. As I work, I think about Caroline and how to approach her.

She seems a little shy, at least around me. I wonder if that's a good sign or a bad one.

The bell on the front door jingles and I look up, smiling

when I see Jacob walking in. He waves at me and I set the box of sweaters down on the counter and head over to him.

"What are you doing here?" I ask him with a smile.

"I came to see if you wanted to grab a late lunch with me, but I'm guessing that you've already been across the street," he says and my eyes flick over his shoulder to the Virgin Street Diner.

"Yeah, I just got back."

"Did you finally ask her out?" he asks, but I know he already knows the answer to that question.

"Not today."

Jacob sighs, hanging his head dramatically.

"She was busy," I try to defend myself and he just groans.

"You're killing me, man."

"I'm killing myself," I mumble.

"Why don't you just bite the bullet and ask her?"

"I just don't want her to reject me."

Jacob mulls over my words and we're silent for a few minutes, both lost in thought. Finally, he comes to a conclusion.

"Why don't you take a break, then? Regroup. You could go up to your cabin for the weekend and decompress. Come back on Monday and have a plan to ask her out or move on. Watching you watching her is getting old, man."

I snort at the last part but I'm sure that he's right. I flip over his words in my head.

Maybe he's right. Maybe a break is just what I need. My subconscious reminds me that Caroline is taking Charlotte camping this weekend and will probably be up near my cabin. I decide to keep that piece of information to myself.

Maybe I'll run into her. Maybe that will be the sign I'm looking for. If I see her, then I'm meant to ask her out and take the leap. If not, then maybe I need to try to get over my infatuation with her.

Infatuation seems like too tame of a word for what I feel for her and I don't think that I'll ever be able to just get over her.

"Yeah, maybe you're right."

"Of course, I'm right," Jacob says with a smile and I laugh at his cocky smile. "I'll leave you to your stocking. Have a nice weekend."

I wave as he heads to the door, letting him know that I'll talk to him on Monday before he heads out the door and across the street to the diner.

I get back to my stocking, all the while wondering if I can really go two whole days without seeing Caroline.

THREE

Caroline

"HURRY, AUNT CAROLINE!" Charlotte cries, racing out to my car.

"I'm coming, I'm coming," I assure her as I drag the last of the camping supplies out and cram it into the small trunk of my car.

Charlotte has been begging to go camping ever since her best friend Monica went a few weeks ago. I don't know the first thing about camping, but how hard could it really be?

I ended up borrowing some sleeping bags, a tent, and some other supplies from Monica's parents. I didn't want to face Heath.

I take one last look around the yard before I close the trunk and head over to the rear passenger door, making sure that Charlotte is all buckled up. We asked Gracie, my best friend in town, if she would stop by and check on the dogs, maybe walk them if she had time while we're gone, and she was more than happy to help. She promised that she would stop by after work tonight, so we should be all set here. It still feels like I'm forgetting something, and I can't shake the feeling as I climb behind the wheel.

"This is going to be so much fun," Charlotte says happily and I can't help but smile and laugh at her obvious excitement.

Growing up in New York, I've never been much of the outdoorsy type, but even I have to admit it's beautiful up here in the Wild Ridge Mountains.

We drive past the Wildflower Falls and then turn and head past the Wild Ridge Fire Ranger Station. I start to worry that we got lost, but then I spot the small yellow sign for the Wild Canyon Camp Sites.

We're immediately swallowed up by the forest and I sigh, trying to figure where to turn. Charlotte is busy telling me about all of the s'mores that she's going to make, and she seems to get more excited the farther into the forest that we drive.

I finally spot the front office and we park outside. Charlotte skips up to the front door, her eyes darting around as she tries to take it all in. It only takes us a few minutes to check in and get our campsite number, and then we're back on our way.

We wind through the campground to our spot in the very back of the acreage. I get turned around at first and end up halfway up the mountain before I realize that we're not in the right location. A lot of these roads aren't labeled clearly and we head back down, finally finding the right spot. We're half hidden in the forest, right at the base of the mountain, and I notice that I can't really see any other tents or campers. It's kind of peaceful, but I still wish that we had neighbors in case I need help with the tent or campfire.

"We're here, bunny!" I say and she bounces excitedly in her car seat.

Her face is practically smashed up against the glass as we turn into our camping site and park. We're one of the only cars out here, and I wonder if we're lucky to have the privacy or if everyone else knows something that I don't.

It's already late afternoon and I know that we're going to need to hurry to set everything up before it gets dark, so I unbuckle Charlotte from her car seat and pop the trunk, dragging out the tent and a chair for her to sit in.

Charlotte immediately starts to wander around the small clearing and I remind her to stay close as I get to work assembling the tent.

It takes me about thirty seconds to realize it's more complicated to put together than I originally thought. I try reading the small instruction pamphlet but it doesn't seem to help.

The sky starts to darken and I chew on my bottom lip. Would it still be considered camping if we just slept on the ground? Or in my car?

I've got one side of the tent up when the first crack of thunder sounds and Charlotte and I both jump. The sky opens up a second later and I abandon the pitiful tent, grab Charlotte and race back to the car.

We're both soaked when we climb in and I start the car, turning the heat all the way up to help dry us off.

"Does this mean that we can't go camping this weekend?" Charlotte asks and I shake my head.

"Not today anyway, bunny. We'll have to try again a different day."

She pouts and I tell her to sit tight as I race back outside and grab up the chair and tent poles. The tent is flapping in the wind and I grab it and wrestle it into the backseat, too.

We'll have to take it home and let it dry out before we give it back to Monica's parents.

Now I know why we were the only people out here camping today, I think as I get Charlotte buckled up in her car seat and put the car in reverse. I want to get back on pavement ASAP so that we don't get stuck in the mud somewhere.

The main road leading up here is gravel, which isn't great, but it's better than the soft campground dirt. I have my hazard lights on and my windshield wipers going at their highest speed, and I can still barely see where I'm going.

"You alright, bunny?" I ask and she nods, looking nervous.

None of my surroundings look familiar and I wonder if it's because I can't see anything or if maybe I took a wrong turn somewhere. I don't have any cell reception, so I can't look up directions.

I slow when I see a house light and decide to pull over and ask for directions. Maybe it will be someone friendly and we can wait out a bit of the storm with them.

I pull into the drive and twist around to look at Charlotte.

"I'm going to go up there and ask for directions, okay? I'll be right back."

She nods, clutching her stuffed bunny to her chest. She must have grabbed it from her backpack when I was collecting the tent.

"Be right back," I promise her as I climb out and race through the storm to the front porch.

I'm sure that I look like a drowned rat by the time that I make it to the front door, and I sigh as I knock. Then I wait.

When no one answers, I wonder if they can hear me over the storm, so I knock again.

I'm just about to turn and head back to the car when the door opens and my mouth drops open.

"Yeah, of course this is your place," I grumble as I push the dripping wet hair out of my face and stare up at Heath Winters.

FOUR

Heath

I MUST BE DREAMING. That's the only way to explain Caroline standing on my front porch, soaking wet.

I had just been missing her and thinking about her, like always, when she knocked on my door. I hadn't heard it over the torrential rain, but I'm glad I heard her the second time.

"Yeah, I live here," I answer her. "Why don't you come in out of the rain?"

I step aside but she hesitates.

"Charlotte is in the car," she says, pointing over her shoulder to her idling car.

"She can come in, too. You shouldn't be driving in this weather anyway."

She bites her lip, debating, and I wait her out.

"Alright," she says before she turns and runs back to her car.

She's back with Charlotte and her backpack a few

minutes later and I smile at the little girl as Caroline sets her on her feet.

"Hi, Mr. Heath," Charlotte says with a smile, running over and wrapping her little arms around my leg. "We were camping."

"I heard. I'm sorry that you got rained on," I tell her and she nods.

"It's okay. We're going to try later."

"Well, let me get you some towels and you can get dry."

Caroline is still hanging out by the front door and I give her a smile before I head to get them some towels. I come back out and can't help but laugh when I see Charlotte digging through her little backpack. She's got a worn stuffed bunny under one arm and a bag of marshmallows under the other.

"Look what we have, Mr. Heath!" Charlotte says excitedly, and I have a feeling that I'll be building a fire so that we can make s'mores at some point tonight.

"Yum! Did you want to make s'mores?"

Charlotte nods, jumping up and down and I wrap a towel around her shoulders before I pass the other one to Caroline.

"You two dry off and I'll get a fire started."

I think I have some dry firewood in the back room, so I head out there. I grab a few logs and rummage around until I find the sticks to roast the marshmallows.

"Do you need any of the stuff out of your car?" I ask Caroline as I crouch down near the fireplace.

"That depends. Do you know how long it's supposed to rain like this?"

"Uh, I think it might be all weekend, actually."

Caroline's shoulders sag and I try to give her a friendly smile.

"You both are welcome to stay here for as long as you want."

"Thanks," Caroline says, taking a few more steps into the cabin.

She starts to look around as Charlotte takes a seat on the couch and tries to open the box of graham crackers. I get the fire started and then head over to the thermostat on the wall and turn the air up so that we aren't all sweltering in a few minutes.

"Ready to make your s'more, bunny?" Caroline asks and Charlotte nods, jumping off the couch.

I help her with the supplies as Caroline picks up the towels and hangs them over the back of a kitchen chair.

"Have you ever toasted marshmallows before?" I ask and they both shake their heads *no*. "No worries, I'll show you how to make the perfect one."

We open the bag of marshmallows and I put one on the stick before I hold it over the fire. I make sure that Charlotte doesn't get too close to the fire. Once the marshmallow is the perfect golden brown, I ask Caroline to pass us some graham crackers and chocolate and we slide the marshmallow between the crackers.

"There you go," I say, passing the s'more over to Charlotte.

She grins at me, taking a big bite of the s'more and immediately getting chocolate and marshmallow all over her face.

"It's good!" Charlotte giggles and takes another bite as I laugh and get started on the next s'more.

I pass the second s'more to Caroline and watch as she takes a bite. She licks a stray smear of marshmallow off her bottom lip and I have to look away before I embarrass myself.

The rain starts to lessen outside, but by now it's pitch black out, and I know that Caroline and Charlotte shouldn't be driving in this weather. I'm also just not ready for our time together to be over. It feels like I'm finally getting Caroline to see me.

"Why don't I get your bags from your car and you can get out of your wet clothes."

There's a beat of awkward silence as we both think about her wet clothes clinging to her in certain places and I clear my throat, looking back toward the fire.

"Okay," Charlotte says happily.

"Thanks," Caroline adds and I could swear that she's blushing.

I grab the car keys from Caroline before she can say anything else or I can get any other ideas, and I head out into the rain to grab their things. I just grab the two small duffle bags from the back seat before I hurry back inside.

Charlotte is looking tired and I pass the bags to Caroline and point them toward the bedroom to get changed. While they do that, I put the fire out and clean up all of the s'mores stuff.

Charlotte pads back out a few minutes later, dressed in her pajamas, and curls up on the couch.

"Are you warm enough?" I ask her and she nods sleepily.

I get up to grab her a blanket from the hall closet and by the time I'm back, she's fast asleep. I cover her up with the blanket and turn to see Caroline watching me.

"There's only the one bedroom. I'll grab Charlotte and you two can take the bed. I'll sleep out here on the couch."

"Are you sure? I don't want to kick you out of your bed after you were nice enough to let us stay here."

"I'm sure, Caroline. It's no problem. Really."

She nods and I gently pick Charlotte up and follow her into the bedroom. Caroline pulls back the covers and I lay Charlotte down, smoothing her hair away from her face before I cover her up with the blanket.

Caroline follows me back to the door and we stare at each other for a moment before I give her a small smile. I lean down and I could swear that Caroline holds her breath as I brush my lips against her cheek.

"Goodnight, Caroline."

"Goodnight, Heath," she whispers back as I straighten and head out to the couch.

I lay down with a smile on my face. Sure, my feet might be hanging over the end of the couch and I can already tell that I'll have a crick in my neck tomorrow morning, but the woman of my dreams is asleep in my bed, and it feels like I just took one big step toward making her mine.

Now to make sure that I don't do anything to mess up my progress.

FIVE

Caroline

"I WISH WE COULD GO CAMPING," Charlotte says glumly as she stares out the window at the rain pouring down outside.

She's said this at least ten times this morning and I'm worried that she's annoying Heath. He went outside about fifteen minutes ago and hasn't come back in.

"I know, bunny. I do, too, but it's still storming out there. We'll have to try to go a different weekend," I tell her.

"Or..." Heath says as he comes in through the back door. "I could set up my tent in here and we could go camping inside."

"Yeah!" Charlotte yells excitedly as she scrambles over to help Heath with the supplies.

I sit on the couch, sipping the coffee Heath made before I even got up this morning and watch them. I'd offer to give him a hand but I know nothing about tents and I'm sure that I would only get in the way.

Charlotte grins over at me as Heath puts the final rod in the tent and I smile back at her. It would have taken me at least four times as long to set up the tent.

"Can we make hot dogs over the fire?" Charlotte asks Heath and he nods.

He made us eggs, bacon, and toast for breakfast this morning and I'm a little concerned that we're going to eat him out of house and home.

"I have some food and stuff in the cooler out in my car," I tell him, standing to head outside to grab it but he's already at the door.

"I'll grab it. I'm already a little wet from getting the tent," he says with a slightly timid smile as he darts outside and over to my car.

It takes him a couple of minutes to dig the cooler out of the car and by the time he's headed back up to the house, he's drenched.

His black T-shirt clings to him and my mouth starts to water at the sight. His hair is plastered to his head and he has drops of rain running down his face.

I want to lick those drops off of him.

I jerk my gaze away from him, looking over to Charlotte as Heath comes back inside. I can't be thinking about Heath like that. I need to get my head on straight here. I just moved to Cherry Falls not that long ago. I need to get settled here, make sure that Charlotte is alright, and make the diner a success before I can even think about dating.

Besides, what if I dated Heath and then we broke up? It would be so awkward to still have to see him every day, and since our businesses are literally across the street from each other, I know we would be running into each other a lot.

I watch as Heath and Charlotte work together to dig the food out of the cooler. He heads back outside and comes back with some campfire cooking sticks and three sleeping bags.

"I'll make you one, Caroline," Charlotte tells me when I move to help them and I laugh.

"Thanks, bunny."

I watch the two of them work together and I'm surprised. I never thought Heath would be good with kids since he seems too gruff with adults, but he's patient and kind as he helps Charlotte with the hot dogs.

"Oh man! I burned it," Charlotte says and I grimace as I think about eating that one.

"I love burned hot dogs," Heath says right away. "Can I have it?"

Charlotte nods, smiling as she holds the stick steady and Heath grabs the now ruined hot dog with a bun. He slathers it in ketchup and mustard and I bite back a smile when I see him take a big bite and only slightly grimace.

When Charlotte looks at him, he takes another big bite, giving her a smile.

"It's delicious. Thanks, Charlotte."

She grins at him, holding up the package of hot dogs for him to help her with it. He slides another hot dog onto the end of her stick and back into the fire it goes. This time, he helps her hold it out of the flames and shows her how to turn the stick so the hot dog cooks evenly. A few minutes later, she has a perfectly cooked hot dog and Heath puts it on a bun for her before he hands it over.

"Now we just need to make one for Caroline."

Heath gets to work on that while Charlotte eats her hot dog and I move over, grabbing a bun to help him when he pulls it away from the flames.

"Thank you," I whisper to him and I hope he knows that I'm thanking him for more than just the hot dog.

I love seeing Charlotte so happy and I love that we were still able to go camping. I owe all of that to the strong, rough around the edges man next to me.

"Anytime, Caroline."

I retreat back to the couch to eat my hot dog. I'm not sure that I trust myself being so close to Heath. I can't deny it any longer. I'm attracted to him. I have been since I first arrived in town, but I need to do what's right for Charlotte now, and I don't think that's dating Heath, or anyone for that matter. Not right now at least.

The rest of the afternoon passes in a blur of s'mores, cleaning up messes, and telling silly ghost stories. Charlotte is too afraid to do them at night, so we all climb into the tent with flashlights and do it at three in the afternoon.

Through it all, Heath is a good sport. He's patient with her, laughing the hardest at her ghost stories that don't make any sense, and helping her clean up when she gets marshmallow all over her face.

I'll admit, it's been nice not having to do everything for Charlotte all by myself. Being a single mom is exhausting and I don't know how anyone does it.

"Should we make more hot dogs for dinner, bunny?" I ask when it's the evening, and she nods.

This time I sit by them on the floor, next to the fire with Charlotte between us. We manage not to burn any of the hot dogs this time, and I'm not sure if it's all the excitement of today, the fire crackling and heating the whole room, the rain pattering on the windows and roof, or a mixture of all those things, but soon Charlotte is starting to doze off.

"She wanted to sleep in the tent," Heath says and I nod, moving to open the flap as he scoops her up in his strong arms.

He cradles her gently against him as we both move into

the tent and tuck her into her sleeping bag. She doesn't even stir and I smile down at her sleeping face, bending over to press a kiss to her forehead

"Goodnight, bunny," I whisper and she sighs, tucking her little fist beneath her chin.

I follow Heath out of the tent and look around the living room. It's a bit of a disaster with candy wrappers, graham cracker crumbs and stray smears of marshmallow on the floor by the fireplace.

"Let me help you clean up," I say, heading past him to where I saw the broom in the kitchen.

"I can get it," he says, trying to stop me.

His hand wraps around my hip and my breath stalls in my lungs as I look up at him. Our eyes meet and cling to each other as we remain motionless.

"Caroline," he whispers and I can't take it any longer.

My whole body feels like it will explode if I don't feel his lips on mine in the next second. Every cell in my body is urging me toward him and I take another step closer.

"Just kiss me already," I whisper back and in the next instant, his lips are on mine.

His lips are a little rough, probably from the wind and rain outside, but I love it. They brush against mine softly, his hands tightening around my waist and pulling me closer.

My hands land on his wide chest and I can feel his heartbeat racing underneath my palm. I can feel every hard plane of his body and when my belly rubs against a certain thick ridge in his pants, I can't hold back my gasp. My panties start to grow damp with my arousal and I step closer to him when suddenly I hear a sound from inside the tent.

Heath and I both jump away from each other as Charlotte sleepily climbs out of the tent.

"I need to go to the bathroom," she says, her eyes barely

open and I avoid Heath's gaze as I help her to the bathroom.

By the time I return, he has the living room cleaned up and is just setting another log on the fire.

"Are you guys coming to bed now?" Charlotte asks and I nod.

"Yeah, I just need to brush my teeth and get into my pajamas."

"Are you coming, Heath?" Charlotte asks sweetly and his eyes dart to mine.

I look away from him, heading into the bedroom to get changed instead. I hurry through brushing my teeth and then pad back out to the living room. I don't see Heath and I wonder if he's in the kitchen as I climb into the tent. There are three sleeping bags lined up inside and Charlotte is already tucked back into the one by the right side wall.

Heath is on the other side, lying on his back, his body tense. He gives me a strained smile as I climb into the sleeping bag in the middle. Charlotte blinks her eyes open at me and I lean over and give her another kiss on her forehead.

"Night, Caroline. Night, Heath," she says, her eyes fluttering closed.

"Night," we both say and then we lie there in silence.

I know he's still awake and I wrack my brain trying to figure out a way to break this tension between us, but all I can focus on is the insistent ache between my legs.

I want him. Bad.

You can't have him. Think about Charlotte. Think about what's best for her.

I sigh, flopping onto my back and staring up at the ceiling. It's really too bad that I can't pursue this thing with Heath because I'm pretty sure I just fell in love with him a little bit this weekend.

SIX

Heath

I BARELY SLEPT LAST NIGHT. Not with Caroline sleeping just a few inches away from me, her sweet clementine scent wrapped around me like a blanket. A few times she rolled over, her sleeping bag inching closer to mine. When her breath fanned over my face, I was rock hard. When the back of her hand brushed against mine, I swear I almost came just from that one innocent touch.

I eventually passed out, only to wake up with her wrapped up tight in my arms, her head resting on my chest, my arms like a vise around her, banding her tight against me.

She had looked up at me, blinking the sleep from her eyes and my heart had started to race so hard that it would be a miracle if she could hear anything else, especially with her ear still pressed against my chest.

I had almost blurted out that I loved her right then and there but had chickened out at the last second. I've barely been able to get her to talk to me. Blurting out that I would do anything to make her mine will probably only scare her away even more.

Caroline hadn't said anything when our eyes met. She seemed more startled than I was that we had apparently cuddled for at least part of last night.

She just rolled over, facing away from me, and I stared up at the ceiling of the tent, wondering what the hell I should do now.

Charlotte had woken up a few minutes after that and since the rain had stopped, they were getting ready to head home. I had insisted on making them breakfast and helping them load up their car again.

Now I'm just standing here, awkwardly staring at Caroline as she shifts in front of me. Charlotte is already buckled into her car seat, busy playing with her stuffed rabbit and happily munching on some graham crackers that I gave her for the car ride.

"Thanks for everything. We both had a lot of fun and I can't thank you enough for letting us stay here with you."

"Anytime," I tell her honestly and then before I can chicken out, I blurt out, "Would you like to go to dinner with me sometime?"

She blinks up at me, obviously caught off guard and I wince internally.

God, I'm so freaking bad at this.

"I kind of have a lot going on with the diner and Charlotte," she starts and I nod.

"I know, but maybe it's about time that you did something for yourself," I say, hoping that I'm not overstepping any boundaries here.

I can see how much of herself she gives to everything and everyone else. She's always so busy with the diner or with helping out someone from town that she never really gives herself a break. I just want to help her relax and hopefully have a little fun in the process.

"Okay," Caroline says after a minute, a shy smile curving her lips.

"Seriously?" I blurt out and she giggles at that.

"Yeah, you're probably right. I should try to work on taking some time for myself."

I can feel the smile threatening to break my face and I will myself to tone it down a bit.

"Good. Does tomorrow night work?"

"Yeah, I should be free. Can we go earlier in the day? Maybe around four pm?"

I would literally move heaven and earth to be with this girl. Cutting out of work a few hours early isn't going to be an issue.

"Yeah, that's fine. I'll pick you up then."

"Okay, I'll see you at four pm then."

I nod as I help get her car door and she slides behind the wheel.

"See you tomorrow," I tell Charlotte and Caroline, waving as she starts the car and starts to back out of the drive.

Charlotte grins, waving back at me as they drive off and I grin, waving back until the car disappears from view.

I head back inside, cleaning up the cabin and locking it down before I head back into town myself. I pass by the Virgin Street Diner, smiling to myself as I think about how different everything feels now that I'm back in town.

I think things are finally starting to go my way.

SEVEN

Caroline

I HADN'T EVEN THOUGHT about getting a babysitter for tonight, so I'm lucky that Gracie stopped into the diner today for lunch and volunteered to watch Charlotte for me tonight. She's the town florist and had promised that closing a little early wouldn't be a problem.

I never really dated much growing up, and I'm so used to hanging out with Charlotte that I hadn't thought about not taking her on our date, but I agreed with Heath that I needed some 'me time', so taking her with us would have defeated the purpose.

"So, she can have macaroni and cheese or I left some money on the kitchen counter if you want to order a pizza or something," I tell Gracie as I grab my purse from the hook by the door.

"We'll be fine!" Gracie promises, her ever-present smile on her face. "Won't we, Charlotte?"

"Yeah!" Charlotte yells and the dogs start barking with her.

Heath knocks on the door a second later and I have to sidestep the dogs to answer it.

"Hey," I greet him, blushing slightly as he passes me a bouquet of flowers that I'm sure he bought from Gracie earlier today.

"Hey," he says, handing me the flowers and grabbing Remy and Rory before the dogs can make it out the door.

"Alright, be good, bunny. I'll be back in a little bit," I promise as I scoop down and grab Charlotte.

She giggles as I hug her, peppering her face with kisses.

"Have fun you two!" Gracie says, waving as she closes the door behind us.

"Ready?" Heath asks, holding his hand out to me and I smile, slipping my hand into his as he leads me over to his truck.

He helps me up and I breathe in deep. His truck smells just like him. Outdoorsy with just a hint of some kind of cologne. It drives me wild.

He buckles up and we start down the quiet streets of Cherry Falls. He heads toward Kissme Bay and I raise an eyebrow at him.

"What?" he asks with a low laugh, one that rumbles along my skin.

"Just surprised that we weren't staying in Cherry Falls."

"Where would we go? The diner for dinner?" he asks with another laugh and I join him.

Cherry Falls is pretty small and the only real date options are the Fireside Bar and Grill, Virgin Street Diner, or the Cherry on Top Ice Cream Parlor.

I try to relax as we head out of town but I'm still a bundle of nerves. Part of me is still worried about leaving

Charlotte for the first time that wasn't school. I know Gracie has it covered, though. She's awesome with kids and I wonder when she'll find someone and settle down.

The bigger part of me is worried that I'm going to embarrass myself and will never be able to show my face around Heath again.

It doesn't take long to reach Kissme Bay since it's the next town over. Heath slows as we enter the town and I look out the window, taking in the different storefronts.

I've haven't been to Kissme Bay before but it's been on my list of places to take Charlotte for a while.

"Mini golf!" I say excitedly as we drive past a place called Dimpled Balls.

"Want to play?" Heath asks and I nod, but he's already pulling into the parking lot.

He helps me out of the truck and we head for the door. There's only one other couple playing right now, and they're already on the seventh hole, so I know that we won't catch up to them.

He pays and I pick out my putter and ball, grabbing another one for Heath. He comes over with a slip of paper and a golf pencil, and I pass him his putter. It isn't until we're on the first hole that I realize how much I missed playing.

"I used to go with my brother all the time in high school," I say, a pang of sadness hitting me.

"So, you're trying to warn me that I'm about to get my butt kicked?" Heath asks and I smile at him, grateful that he's trying to lighten the mood again.

"Oh yeah," I say with a laugh, hitting my ball and watching as it rolls down the green, banking off of the wall, and rolling to a stop a few inches from the hole.

Heath groans and I grin, walking over and easily putting

it in. He marks my score down on the card before he shoves the paper and pencil back in his pocket.

He bends down, setting up his ball, and when he stands up to putt, I can't help but laugh. I swear that his arms are longer than the putter and he's crouched down so low that he's practically at a ninety-degree angle. I can see him grinning as he hits the ball.

He hit it way too hard and it goes sailing over to the green on the next hole.

"Just want to remind you that we're still on the first hole," I joke and he laughs, heading over to hit his ball again.

The rest of the game continues that way. I don't think Heath makes a hole without hitting it at least ten times and by the time we're done, his score is three times higher than mine.

"Thanks, that was a lot of fun," I say, grinning up at him and he laughs.

"Yeah, it was."

I love that he can take a joke and he isn't super competitive. I don't know why I thought he would be. Heath is the literal definition of a gentle giant.

"What should we do next?" he asks and I check my watch, surprised to see that we spent close to an hour and a half playing mini golf.

"Can we grab something to eat?"

"Of course," he says, taking my hand in his and leading me over to the Reef Beach Bar.

The place is right across from the water and everything in it seems to be painted some neon color. Heath pulls out a neon pink stool for me and I hop on, watching as he takes the neon green one beside me.

The waitress comes over to take our orders a few minutes later and we both get burgers with a Coke.

"You've lived in Cherry Falls all of your life, right?" I ask him, taking a sip of my drink.

"Yeah," he says with a nod, his eyes locked on my mouth wrapped around my straw and my body starts to tingle as his eyes heat.

"You've probably been here a million times then, huh?"

"Not really. I used to come with Jacob sometimes, but I was always more of a loner. I'd rather be up in the mountains camping or something than around all of these people."

I nod. He did seem more comfortable up in the woods than in this crowded bar.

"What about you?" Did you go to a lot of places like this when you were younger?"

"Well, I'm from New York City, so besides Coney Island, there really aren't that many places like this in the city. My friends Sayler and Coraline would drag me out there sometimes but I always felt like a third wheel."

"Why is that?" Heath asks with a frown.

"They were always like sisters. I met them when we were freshman in high school, and by then they had been best friends for close to a decade. It's hard to compete with that kind of history."

Our food comes and we both dig in.

"What did you like to do at Coney Island?" he asks after a minute.

"The arcade," I answer right away, smiling as I remember the flashing lights and laughing as we tried to beat each other.

Sayler was terrible at the games. She'd get distracted and she'd rather be moving than just sitting there pretending to drive a race car, but Coraline and I loved it.

"We should go to Holidaze Arcade after this," he suggests and I nod.

"Only if you're sure," I say and he looks confused.

"Why wouldn't I be?"

"I was just worried that you were sick of losing to me already," I joke and he grins.

"Never."

We finish our food and Heath pays before we head back to the truck. The arcade is actually right across from the mini golf place. Heath parks and I race him inside, laughing as he picks me up before I can reach the door.

"Cheater!" I cry as he enters first and he laughs.

We grab some tokens and Heath follows me around as I check out all of the games. When I find the racing one, I grin, taking a seat. Heath crams himself into the seat next to me and I smile as I put my tokens in.

We're more evenly matched in the arcade and by the time we're out of tokens, we're both tired and my side hurts from laughing so much.

"Come on. One more stop," he says, taking my hand and crossing the road.

We walk over to Frenchie's Ferris Wheel. It's all lit up now and I realize that another three hours have passed without me realizing it. It feels good to go so long without worrying about Charlotte, the diner, or anything else.

"What made you decide on taking me here for our date?" I ask Heath as we take our seats on the Ferris wheel and start to rise into the air.

"It just felt like you hadn't had much fun in a while. You're always working so hard, and I rarely see you smile. I just wanted to do something to make you happy."

My heart dips in my chest at that. Heath starts to blush

and I realize that I've just been staring at him for a solid minute.

"Besides," he says, clearing his throat, "I wanted to be prepared. I wasn't sure if you were bringing Charlotte or not and if you did, I wanted her to have fun, too."

That does it.

Hearing him say that has me falling for him right then and there and I can't help it. I lean over, my lips brushing against his as we continue to rise into the sky.

EIGHT

Heath

WALKING into the Virgin Street Diner the next day feels so different. This time, when I walked into the diner, Caroline smiled at me, her cheeks heating slightly and I wonder if she was thinking about our kiss from last night.

I took my seat at the counter, grinning as Caroline set my usual glass of water down in front of me. I have to hold myself back from grabbing her, dragging her across the counter and kissing her, and I think she knows. She winks at me, turning and heading back into the kitchen to place my order and I watch her go.

Even though we went to the next town over for our date last night, I'm sure that at least half of the town has already heard about it. To be honest, I can't wait for everyone to know about the two of us but I have a feeling that Caroline wants to talk to Charlotte about it before the gossip hits her. I've never really dated before but I imagine that adding a kid to the mix changes things.

"Hey, Heath," Ken says.

He's the town doctor and he must be on his lunch break.

"Hey, how's it going?" I ask, taking in the dark circles under his eyes.

"Good, keeping busy," he says, rubbing at his eyes. He looks like he's about two seconds away from taking a nap on the counter.

"Hey, Heath," Gracie says, smiling conspiratorially at me as she takes the seat on the other side of Ken.

"Hey, what can I get you two?" Caroline asks as she sets my food down in front of me and moves to take Ken and Gracie's order.

"Coffee," Ken croaks and I see Gracie shoot him a sympathetic look.

"I'll take a BLT and a slice of that pie," Gracie says, pointing over to the cherry pie in the case.

"That sounds good. Make it two," Ken says, not even bothering to lift his head from the counter.

I eat my lunch, sharing looks across the diner with Caroline any chance I can. She stops to talk to me whenever she gets the chance, too, but it's not enough. Ken and Gracie both left and I need to get back to the Trading Post soon but I can't go. Not yet. Not until I get another taste of my sweet girl.

When it looks like everyone is busy, I slip behind the counter and head down the hallway toward the back office I just saw Caroline head into.

I close the door behind me and smile as Caroline stands and makes her way around the desk.

"Hey," I whisper and she giggles.

"Hey. Why are we whispering?"

"It just felt right," I tell her, enjoying the sound of her laughter.

"You know what else would feel right?" she asks, her hands on my chest as she leans up on her toes.

"Uh huh," I whisper back, my lips meeting hers in a gentle caress.

Her hands land on my shoulders, squeezing there before she reaches up, tangling her fingers in my hair and pulling me closer to her. I cup the back of her head, wanting us closer, too.

She moans into my mouth when my tongue slides across her lips. The kiss is soft, sweet, and unrushed, and I love it. I lick the seam of her mouth once more, asking her to let me come inside. She surrenders with a moan, parting for me and giving us what we both want.

"Caroline? The meat delivery is here!" Amelia calls and we break apart, both of us breathing heavy.

We don't pull away immediately, but I know she has to get back to work, so I drop one last kiss on her lips before I step back.

"Have dinner with me again."

"Okay. Later this week? Maybe Friday or Saturday?"

"Perfect," I say, stealing one last kiss. "Why don't I take you both out tomorrow though. I can't last until Friday without seeing you."

Caroline smiles wide at that and I love seeing her look so happy.

"Alright, if you insist."

"I do," I say as I take her hand and we head back out into the diner with her.

She waves goodbye at me as I head for the door, and I practically skip all the way across the street back to the Cherry Falls Trading Post.

I'm surprised to find my old friend Graham waiting for me outside of the Trading Post when I get back from lunch.

"Hey, man. I didn't know that you were in town," I say as we hug and clap each other on the back.

"Just passing through and thought I would stop in and say hi, see if you wanted to grab lunch or something."

"Oh, I just ate, but I can grab a cup of coffee or something with you if you want."

"Nah, let's just head inside and catch up. I can grab something when I head out of town."

I unlock the shop's door and lead him inside.

"Do you need anything?" I ask him as he looks around the place.

Graham lives up in the mountains on Fallen Peak. I don't know much about his past but he stops by town every few months and we always catch up.

"Maybe. I'll have to look around. I've got to stock up before winter hits and we all get snowed in up there."

"We got some new camping gear in. There's some cool gas griddles that we just got in."

Graham nods as he leans over, resting on the front counter.

"How are things going with you? Did you ever make a move on your diner dream girl?" he asks with a smile.

"As a matter of fact, yes I did. We just had our first date and we're going out again in a few days."

"Congratulations."

"Thanks, what about you? Any special lady in your life?" I ask and he snorts out a laugh as he shakes his head.

"No, there's not a lot of eligible bachelorettes in Fallen Peak."

"Maybe you'll find someone down here," I suggest.

"Maybe," he says but I can tell he doesn't really believe it.

Some tourists come in then, and Graham wanders off to check out some of the camping gear. I move over to help them, and seeing the hiking boots gives me an idea for my next date with Caroline.

I check them out and then help Graham check out and haul his supplies out to his Jeep.

"I'll see you next time you're in town," I say as I shake his hand and he nods.

"See you then. You can catch me up on diner girl."

"Sounds good."

I wave as he drives away. It only takes a second for me to get distracted when I spot Caroline through the front windows of the diner. She waves at me, grinning, and I wave back before I head back inside my shop.

I think about Caroline for the rest of the afternoon. I grab some hiking boots that I think will fit her and Charlotte and stack them behind the counter for later. I can't wait to spend more time with her.

It feels so right being with her. It's effortless and that's how I know that we were meant to be.

Now I just need to convince her of that.

NINE

Caroline

I SMILE down at my new hiking boots as I trail behind Heath and Charlotte on the well-worn trail. Heath surprised both of us with the boots when he picked us up a few hours ago. Charlotte loves hers with the pink laces and she couldn't wait to put them on.

I had heard of the falls up in Wild Ridge Mountains but never thought of taking Charlotte there. Being back in the mountains reminds me of the camping trip and I can't help but grin.

Charlotte is holding onto Heath's hand, chattering about everything that she sees and Heath is patiently listening to her. She's very excited about the possibility of seeing some bunnies out in the wild and I hope that we can find some.

This hiking trail is super easy and only about half a mile long but that doesn't stop Charlotte from asking if Heath can carry her. He obliges, letting her ride on his shoulders so that she can get a better view.

My heart clenches as I see the two of them together. It's been a huge adjustment becoming a single mom and there have been a lot of times that I would have done anything for some help.

I was always too afraid to bring anyone around Charlotte, though. She had just lost most of her family and the therapist had warned me about bringing people into her life that wouldn't stay.

I needed to find people who were in it for the long haul and I think that's Heath.

I hope that it's Heath.

We come out in front of the falls, close to the spray, and I laugh as Charlotte giggles, wiggling on Heath's strong shoulders.

"Want down?" he asks her, one of her tiny hands in his, keeping her steady.

"Not yet. I like being taller than everyone else," she says with a giggle and he laughs.

We walk along the edge and eventually Charlotte wants down. She holds onto Heath's hand as she leans over, dipping her fingers into the cool water.

"Are you hungry?" Heath asks as we start to hike back.

"Yeah!" Charlotte yells.

"There's a little café around the corner that we can go to."

"Sounds good," I say as we head back to the car.

We didn't see any rabbits on our outing and Charlotte was a little upset, but Heath promised to take us back to his cabin and said we could hike around and look for some there. She seems to have forgotten all about her disappointment, though, as Heath carries her back to our car.

I strap her into her car seat and try not to laugh as Heath tries to fit his large frame into my little car. I have a feeling he'll be buying a car seat for his truck very soon so that we don't have to move mine or keep taking my car out when we're together.

We make the short drive around the corner to the Pine Cone Café. It's a cute little place nestled back by the forest and mountains.

It's after the lunch rush so the place isn't that busy as we head inside. We sit down at one of the wooden tables and Charlotte scoots close to Heath on the bench seating. The place is rustic with animal heads on the wall and plaid curtains and seat cushions.

"What are you hungry for, bunny?" I ask as I grab one of the menus off the table.

"Can I have pancakes?"

"I'm not sure if they're doing breakfast anymore."

"We can ask," Heath says and I smile as he flags down Aspen, the owner of the café.

"Sure, we can make you some pancakes, sugar," Aspen says with a smile and Charlotte bounces in her seat.

"I'll take the burger and a Coke," I say as I slide my menu back in the holder.

"That sounds good. Me too. Thanks, Aspen," Heath says as she writes down our order and heads back toward the kitchen.

"Have you been here before?" I ask him and he nods.

"Yeah, sometimes I stop by on my way to or from my cabin. The food is always good."

"Have you ever ordered the pancakes?" Charlotte asks Heath and I watch as he leans over and talks with her.

"Yeah, and the egg sandwich. They're both really good. Do you like eggs?"

The two of them talk and my heart feels like it's beating out of rhythm. Charlotte was always super close with her dad. The two of them were practically inseparable and watching her and Heath bond has me wondering if he's good for more than just me.

Charlotte giggles, grinning up at Heath and it's obvious that she likes spending time with him. He's so good with her. So patient and easy going.

I used to think of him as the grumpy guy who snapped at me the first time he came into the diner, but he's opened up with us so much since that first meeting. Maybe he was just having a bad day. He's not the gruff loner that the rest of the town seems to think he is. At least not with me.

He's funny, intelligent, and kind. He makes me laugh, makes me take time for myself, and is a great role model for Charlotte.

He's perfect and I think that I might be falling for Heath.

Aspen comes back and sets our food down in front of us, but my stomach is tied up in knots at my revelation and I watch as the two of them dig into their food.

When did that happen? We haven't been together for that long, so I must just be getting ahead of myself.

As he leans over and wipes a stray smear of cheese from her face, I realize that it's more than that.

I'm already in love with Heath.

TEN

Heath

"THANKS FOR TAKING US OUT TODAY," Caroline says as she lets Charlotte into the house.

Rory and Remy are barking and going crazy, trying to lick Charlotte's face. She laughs and runs off, her stuffed bunny clutched tight in her hand.

"Anytime. I had a lot of fun."

"Us too," she says, stepping closer to me and my heart starts to race.

"Me too," I whisper as her hands rest on my chest and she giggles.

Real smooth, Heath. Why don't you tell her how much fun you had one more time just to make sure she heard you?

She smiles, rising up on her tiptoes and I meet her halfway. Our lips connect and everything else in the world disappears. There's just Caroline and me.

The kiss goes slow, like we're both trying to memorize

and learn the taste and feel of the other. Then she moans and I lose all control.

Hearing that sound drives me wild, and I forget all about where we are or that Charlotte is running around nearby. I push my tongue into her mouth, taking everything that she has to give me.

We both get caught up in the intoxicating rush of our kiss, and like a drug addict, I can't resist her. I never want to stop kissing Caroline.

Dogs barking break into my thoughts and Caroline pulls away, her face flushed as she blinks and steps back. I start to follow her before I realize that Charlotte might be close by, and I don't want her to see the bulge in my jeans after making out with her aunt.

"You know, Charlotte has a sleepover at her friend's house Friday night," Caroline says, her voice coming out husky and my cock leaks precum in my jeans. "Want to come over here and keep me company? I could order us some pizza and we could watch a movie or something."

My brain snags on the *or something* in that sentence and I can feel my cock starting to swell even more in my jeans.

Does she mean what I think she means? Or is that just wishful thinking?

"Sure, sounds like fun. What time and what do you like on your pizza? I'll pick it up on my way over."

"Pepperoni and how about six pm? I drop her off at five."

"Sounds good. I'll see you tomorrow at the diner."

"Night," Charlotte says, brushing another kiss across my lips before she turns and heads inside to Charlotte and the dogs.

"Night," I say, turning and heading back to my truck.

The whole way back to my house, I can't stop smiling. I know that we haven't been dating for long, but I already can't imagine my life without her and Charlotte in it.

I go to the diner every day for lunch that week, and I realized that if I go after the lunch rush, Caroline will sit and eat with me. So now I go later so we can spend some more time together.

Then after lunch, we usually go back to her office and make out against the door or her desk until I'm sure that I'm going to bust in my pants.

We might have only been on two official dates, but it feels like I've known her forever. We just click together perfectly.

I wonder if Caroline can tell that I'm already in love with her.

I'm pretty sure that Charlotte can tell. She asked if I was going to marry Caroline today at lunch while Caroline was in the bathroom, and I didn't want to lie to her, so I told her yes. Charlotte had squealed at that but I swore her to secrecy.

I'm just as in love with Charlotte as I am with Caroline, although in different ways. It's impossible not to love the little girl and if I'm not careful, I'm going to end up buying her a dozen rabbits. I wonder if she knows yet just how wrapped around her finger I am.

I head back to my shop, wanting to do some inventory so that I can leave work early on Friday. Nothing is going to keep me from my date with Caroline.

ELEVEN

Caroline

"HIS NAME IS HEATH," I tell Sayler and Coraline as I drive back from dropping Charlotte off at her friend's house for their sleepover.

"How did you meet?" Coraline asks and I think back to the first time I met Heath.

We hadn't exactly become fast friends but I can't deny that I've always been drawn to him. My body always got flushed and all tingly whenever he walked into the diner, and whenever I could feel his eyes on me.

"He's a regular at the diner," I tell them and they *aww*.

"I can't wait to meet him! Are you guys coming on the trip? Rooney said he found a cabin big enough for all of us," Sayler says and I bite my bottom lip.

Is it too soon to be thinking about taking trips together?

My body and my heart both say no. They want him and they don't want to go slow. I've seen how good he is with

Charlotte and there's no denying that he makes me laugh and that I have fun with him.

Can I really rush into this? Just let my emotions guide me?

"I'll have to ask him," I say, biting my lip.

I feel like a teenager, planning trips with my boyfriend and talking to my friends about him.

"I should go. I need to clean up before he gets here," I tell my friends and they both say they'll talk to me soon before we end the call.

I hang up, smiling as I drive back through Cherry Falls toward my house. It took longer than I thought to drop Charlotte off at her friend's house and now I'm running late. Heath is supposed to be here in half an hour and I still have so much to get done. I know that we're just hanging out at my place, but I still wanted to look nice and I need to clean up the place a little bit.

I pull into the driveway, slam my car into park and hurry inside. The house is even messier than I remember and I bend down, scooping up all of Charlotte's toys and stuffed animals into the cubbies of her toy stand in the living room.

My next stop is my bedroom upstairs. I'm like a cyclone as I move around the room, tossing dirty clothes into the hamper and stray shoes into the closet. By the time I'm done, I have ten minutes to hop in the shower, rinse off, and get dressed.

I manage to do it in nine.

I'm headed down the stairs when Heath knocks on the front door. My heart takes off like a shot in my chest and I have to take a deep breath to calm down before I head over to open the front door.

"Hey," I say shyly as I open the door and see Heath standing there.

"Hey, you look gorgeous," he says, ducking his head slightly as he steps inside.

"Thanks. That smells so good," I say as the garlic, tomato, and cheese scent from the pizza boxes in his arms hits me.

"Pepperoni and cheese."

"My favorite," I say, leading him into the kitchen.

"Mine too. Where are the pups?" he asks, just as they start barking at the back door.

"Are you sure you want me to let them in? It's pretty crazy and hectic with them both inside."

"Yeah, I'm sure," Heath says, his eyes holding mine in their gaze.

It feels like he's saying yes to so much more than just letting the dogs in and I smile to myself as I open the back door and let the dogs in.

They run right past me and make a beeline for Heath. I expect him to be a little overwhelmed but he just smiles, bending down and giving each of them some attention.

Watching him grin down at the dogs, his big strong hands running over their fur, I've never wanted to be a dog so bad in my life.

"Are you hungry?" I ask, heading over to the kitchen cabinet and grabbing two plates.

"Yeah," he says his voice husky as he stands.

I can feel my panties starting to grow damp as I set the plates down on the counter, his arm brushing against mine as he joins me.

Suddenly I'm hungry for so much more than food.

"Do you like cold pizza?" I ask him and he stares at me, confused.

"Uh, sure."

"Good," I say, jumping up into his arms.

The action takes him off guard but he has fast reflexes. His hands cup the back of my thighs, his pupils dilating as my legs wrap around his waist and my fingers tangle in his hair.

"Do you want me?" I whisper against his lips and he nods.

"More than I want my next breath. More than anything."

I can't hold back how I feel for him any longer and our lips meet. Kissing him is like jumping out of a plane or being on a rollercoaster. I'm alive. It's the only time lately when I don't feel any of my responsibilities pressing down on me. When I don't feel so completely alone and out of my depth.

Heath kisses me slow and I appreciate him not wanting to rush me but I feel like if I don't feel his skin against mine in the next minute, I'm going to lose my mind.

"Bedroom," I breath and he nods, gripping my hand and leading me toward the stairs.

We take them two at a time and I giggle as he tries to lead me into the bathroom.

"This one," I say, tugging him into my room.

Heath's hands land on my ass and he squeezes as his lips find mine. We back up toward the bed. I can feel his cock, hard and thick just behind the ridge of his zipper, and I moan, wiggling against it as the back of my legs hit the bed.

I reach for his shirt, my fingers clumsy as I try to pull it off of him but he helps me. Our lips break apart and then meet again hungrily as soon as the material is off.

His chest is covered in a dusting of hair and I can't help

but run my hands all over him. I love how hard and strong he is under my palms and I try to rub myself against him.

Heath bites back a groan, breaking the kiss and tugging my shirt off. My bra disappears next and there's only a moment for me to feel self-conscious. It disappears as soon as I catch sight of Heath's face.

His eyes are heated as they devour me. He looks like a man who has found a treasure and is about to fight to the death to keep it.

"Beautiful," he says, his voice gruff as he reaches out and runs one calloused finger down the base of my neck, between my breasts.

He circles my belly button and I shiver.

"Am I your first?" he asks, his voice deeper than it was just a second ago and I nod.

"Yeah, I uh, well, I never got around to it."

The excuse sounds lame but Heath seems pleased.

"Good. I'm your first, then...and your last."

His hands find my pants and he unbuttons them, tugging them and my panties down my legs. As soon as I step out, he pushes me back onto the bed and comes down over me.

I don't know when he pushed his own jeans and boxers down, and I don't worry about it too much. Not when his hot cock rubs against my slit and drives me wild.

"Please," I beg, not even sure what I'm begging for.

"Not yet. I need to get you ready for me first," he says and with that, he starts to kiss his way down my body.

He reaches my breasts and he cups them in his big hands, squeezing them together as he sucks one of my nipples into his mouth. He pulls the pebbled peak between his teeth and I gasp. It feels like there's an electric current straight from my nipples to my core and I clench around nothing.

"I need..." I start but I can't find the words.

"I know what you need," he says, switching to my other nipple and I moan, arching up against his mouth.

I'm writhing beneath him, trying to find something to take the ache between my legs away. I'm just about to beg Heath again when he releases my breasts and starts to kiss lower.

I watch his dark head of hair as he leaves wet kisses over the slight swell of my stomach. He settles between my legs, nudging my thighs further apart so there's room for his wide shoulders.

"So wet," he murmurs as his fingers come up to spread my folds.

My face heats and I'm about to try to close my legs or cover my dripping pussy when Heath leans forward and licks a path up my center.

"Oh, fuck," I moan, drawing the word out as my head falls back against the bed.

Heath chuckles against my skin and I shiver, wiggling my hips to try to get him to do that again.

"My girl has got a delicious, greedy little cunt," he says and I can hear the smile in his voice.

He licks me again, slipping his tongue slightly inside my snug hole and my head thrashes against the mattress. He slips one finger inside of me, pushing it in and out and my hips start to move, learning his rhythm.

"Look at that. Clinging so tight to my finger."

I barely hear his words now, too lost in sensations.

Heath licks me again, this time hitting that little pearl that cause me to see stars. When he sucks it into his mouth, lashing it with his tongue, I'm worried that I might actually black out or go hoarse from screaming.

I claw at his head, my hips restless on the bed as he pushes another finger into me, curling them and rubbing against some secret spot inside of me that has me flying over the edge.

I come against his face and he just keeps licking me.

"More," I say, my voice hoarse and Heath nods, licking his fingers clean.

He pushes his jeans and boxers the rest of the way off and my mouth waters as I get a look at his cock.

I reach out, my fingers wrapping around him and he hisses in a breath.

"You want to explore me?"

"Uh huh," I say, sitting up on the bed and wrapping my fingers tighter around his length.

"That's it," he groans, his eyes dark as he watches me jerk him off.

"Can I taste it?" I ask and his head falls back like he's in pain.

"You never have to ask if you can suck my cock, baby. It's yours now. You can do any fucking thing that you want with it."

I smile, feeling emboldened as I lean forward and take a lick across the head of his cock.

Heath's hands tighten into fists as I open my mouth wider, taking the head of his dick into my mouth and sucking.

"More," he groans and I happily oblige.

I take as much of him as I can, my hand moving up and down on the remaining inches. I find a rhythm and I feel him start to swell in my mouth. I try to pick up my pace but

Heath stops me, pulling me off of him and moving me higher up the bed.

"I'll come down your pretty throat later. Right now, I just need to fill this pussy."

I spread my thighs wide for him in invitation and he grins, fisting his cock and lining it up with my opening.

"Just breathe. I don't want to hurt you," he says and I nod, trying to relax as he starts to push in.

I feel the pinch of pain when he breaks through my virginity and then he's kissing me, his fingers playing with my nipple as he tries to distract me from the pain.

It doesn't hurt anymore. Instead, there's just this pressure inside of me. I need more.

"Move," I moan and Heath balances on his hands, starting to rock slowly in and out of me.

It feels so good. He's so big, stretching me so wide around him as he thrusts in and out of me. I move my legs up, hooking my ankles around his back and it changes the angle, makes it deeper.

I moan when he hits that spot inside of me that feels like I've just been plugged into a socket.

"That's it. Fucking strangle my cock with that tight pussy," Heath growls and his words only drive me higher.

My tits bounce with each hard thrust and Heath groans, his eyes watching the swaying mounds.

"So fucking sexy. Been dreaming about this body for months."

I gasp, my peak hitting hard and I scream as I come around his pulsing length. He thrusts twice more and then I feel him spill inside of me as he finds his own release.

He rolls us over so that I'm sprawled out on top of him and I smile drowsily, nuzzling against his chest.

"That was..." I start, trying to find a word that adequately describes what I just felt.

"Perfect," Heath supplies and I grin.

"Yeah, it was perfect."

His arms wrap around me and we lie like that for a few minutes. When my stomach growls, I start to giggle and Heath rolls me onto my side.

"I got so distracted, I forgot to feed you. Be right back."

I collapse back against my pillows with a smile on my face, feeling boneless. Heath comes back into the room a minute later, a pizza box in his hand and I laugh as he hops back into bed and presents the pizza to me with a flourish.

"Dinner is served," he says and I laugh.

"It looks delicious."

We both take a slice of the now cold pizza and I smile softly as I take a bite, resting my head on Heath's shoulder.

An image of more days like this in the future hits me and I'm surprised at how badly I want that.

I want a future with Heath.

I want everything with Heath.

TWELVE

Heath

"YOU REALLY BOUGHT A CAR SEAT," Caroline says with a bright smile the next day as I help her into my truck.

"Yeah, no offense, but I'm just a little too big for your car. I got the same one that you have and I took it by the firehouse so they could make sure I had it installed correctly."

"Thanks," Caroline says as I back out of the driveway.

I take Caroline's hand in mine as we drive a few blocks over to Charlotte's friend Amelia's house. I can't stop thinking about the things the two of us did together last night and again this morning in the shower.

The first thought I had since I woke up was about getting another taste of that sweet pussy. I rolled Caroline onto her back and buried my face in her folds. I'm pretty sure she was coming before she even fully woke up.

She returned the favor, and by then we were running late and decided to share a shower together. Seeing her curvy body wet and covered in suds had my cock standing at attention and it wasn't long before we were both wrapped around each other again. I took her hard against the wall and then we were really running late.

"I'll go get her. Be right back!" Caroline says, her wet hair still slightly dripping onto her shirt as she unbuckles and hops out of the truck.

I watch her head up to the front door and a second later she disappears into the house. I can't help but smile. Everything is going great. I have the woman that I love and we just spent the entire night wrapped around each other.

I wanted to tell her last night how I felt but I was worried that it would scare her off. I don't want to lose her, so I bit my tongue, but I have a feeling that those three little words will spill out soon.

It doesn't take Caroline long to come back out with Charlotte in tow. I get out to help the little girl into her new car seat and I pass her the stuffed bunny that I got for her.

"Thanks, Heath," she whispers and I frown, wondering if maybe I got the wrong one.

She cuddles it close to her chest, though, so I pass it off, figuring that she's probably just tired from her sleepover or maybe she missed Caroline last night.

"Do you want to go grab some breakfast, Charlotte?" I ask and she nods again, her little eyes falling partly closed and I smile, closing the door.

Maybe she'll sleep on the way over to the café and be back to the excited girl that I'm used to.

"Is the café okay?" I ask Caroline as we head toward the center of town.

"Sure, or I can just make us something at the house."

"Let me spoil you two," I tell her and she blushes slightly, but nods.

"Alright, let's go."

I take her hand again as we drive and we try to ask Charlotte about her sleepover but she doesn't seem interested in talking that much. I can see Caroline frown at her niece as we park and I squeeze her hand.

She seems to shrug it off and we head inside to grab a bite to eat, but things don't improve over breakfast.

"You're not hungry? Did you eat at Amelia's?" Caroline asks as Charlotte takes a few more bites of her pancakes.

"Yeah," she says.

"Are you tired, bunny?"

"Yeah," she says, her eyes drooping and I smile reassuringly at Caroline as I ask for the bill.

"I'll pay. Why don't you go get her settled in her car seat and then I can drive you guys home."

"Thanks," Caroline says as she picks up Charlotte and I watch them head toward the front door.

It only takes a minute for me to pay and I hurry outside to join them. Charlotte is dozing in her car seat by the time I buckle up and pull out of the parking spot.

"It was her first sleepover. I think she must have overdone it and stayed up late."

"Probably. You'll have to take it easy today."

"Yeah, I might need a nap after last night, too," Caroline says with a giggle and I grin.

"Me too."

"We'll have to do it again soon."

"Name the time," I say as I pull into their driveway. "Let me help you carry her in. We can put her right in bed if you want."

"Thanks," Caroline says and I hop out and round the truck to grab Charlotte.

Caroline opens the door for me as I carry Charlotte in. I follow her upstairs and she moves the covers back as I lay her down. She takes Charlotte's shoes off and I watch her as she cares for her niece.

"You're such a good mom. I don't know how you do it all," I tell her as we step out of the bedroom and into the hall.

"Thanks. Most days I'm not sure how I do it all."

"It's inspiring," I say as we stop by the front door.

"It's nice having some help," she admits and I smile, cupping her face in my hand.

"Anytime. I want to help in any way I can."

She smiles, leaning up on her tiptoes so that our lips can meet. I bend down, meeting her halfway, wanting to feel her lips on mine again.

Our lips connect in a heated kiss, our tongues tangling together in an erotic dance and I never want to stop kissing her. I'm lost in the kiss, lost in Caroline, and I never want to be found.

She rubs her chest against mine and I groan when I feel how hard her nipples are. I wonder if she's wet for me; if I reached into her panties, would she be wet for me?

I hope so. I want to feel her juices coating me.

Charlotte groans in her bed and we both pull back. I can see that Caroline is concerned.

"I should go check on that."

"I know," I say, but neither of us makes a move to untangle ourselves. I think that we're both waiting to see if she fell back asleep or not. When there isn't another sound from inside the bedroom, we look back to each other.

Our faces move closer until our lips are molded together once more. I wrap my hand around the back of her neck, holding her close to me and she melts against my chest.

"Caroline?" Charlotte calls, and I pull back, this time taking a step back to avoid the temptation.

I know that she needs to take care of Charlotte so I should leave now before we get lost in each other again. One kiss with Caroline is never enough but I have a feeling kissing Caroline for days wouldn't be enough.

"I'll let you get back to it," I say and she nods as she smooths her hair down.

"We need to get some more alone time."

"Couldn't agree more," I say right away and Caroline laughs. "I'll see you at lunch tomorrow," I say as she opens the door and she smiles.

"See you then."

I smile the whole way home as I think about the future that I'm building with Caroline and Charlotte.

THIRTEEN

Caroline

IT'S lunchtime on Monday and I'm almost giddy as I wait for Heath to come in for our daily lunch date and make out session. I can't stop smiling as I wipe down the counter, keeping one eye on the front door.

I get a rush out of sneaking off with him for a few minutes, and it's like I'm finally getting the wild childhood that I never had. I was always busy with friends, family, and work growing up and to be honest, I always felt like an adult in a teenager's body.

Now, with Heath, I get to feel like a kid again. We're doing fun things like mini golf and Ferris wheel rides and sneaking off to make out together.

Heath grins as we lock eyes through the front window and my heart starts to race.

"Hey, Amelia, I'm going to take a——"

"Break. Yeah, I know," she says with a knowing smile

I just laugh as I set my towel on the back counter and

head over to our usual booth. We slide in across from each other at the same time and Heath reaches for my hand right away.

"How's Charlotte?" he asks and I melt at how concerned he is for her.

He texted me last night and again this morning to see how she was doing and if we needed anything.

"She seems better. She napped for a bit yesterday, so I think she was just overtired from the big sleepover."

"Good," he says and his shoulders seem to relax.

"What have you been doing this morning?" I ask as Amelia sets down our usual order in front of us.

We talk about our mornings as we eat. I got my weekly produce shipment in this morning so it was busy putting all of that away. Heath got in some new camping gear that he's really excited about.

"I should get back to work," I say and I can't help the mischievous smile from curving my lips.

"Yeah, me too."

Heath drops some bills on the table, even though I keep telling him that he doesn't need to pay, but he still keeps leaving money.

He follows after me down the back hallway and into my office. As soon as the door closes, I turn and jump into his arms. My legs wrap around his waist as our mouths fuse together.

Our lips mold together in a heated kiss, our tongues fighting for dominance.

Heath's hands grip my thighs and then he turns, pinning me against the door as he grinds against me. I wore a skirt today for just this reason and I grin against Heath's mouth as his fingers slip further up my thighs, beneath the fabric and he finds me wet and ready.

"Are you needy for me, baby?" he whispers against the shell of my ear.

I nod, goosebumps rising on my arms as I wait to see what he'll do next.

His hands reach for the hem of my shirt and he pulls it off, tossing it behind his back. It lands on my desk and my bra follows soon after.

He keeps me pinned to the door as he unzips his jeans and pulls his cock out, the heavy rod pointing straight up between us.

"Ready?" Heath asks again, his fingers testing my folds and I nod enthusiastically.

Having lunch with him always gets me worked up. I think it's because I know that soon we get to sneak back here and get each other off. It's like a Pavlovian response now. I'm conditioned to want him.

He lines up at my entrance and starts to lower me onto his length. I can't help it. As soon as the first inch is in me, I start to wiggle and rock my hips. Heath just grins at me as I try to work him into me.

"That's it. Work that little pussy down on me. Take it all."

I gush at his words, sinking down another inch.

"Fuck," Heath hisses as my wet heat envelopes him. "We have to be quick. Your staff loves to interrupt us," he groans and I nod, dying to feel him move in me.

He starts up a furious pace, pounding into me as we both cling to each other. His mouth is all over me, licking up my neck, biting under my ear, molding to my mouth and stealing my breath.

I'm surrounded by Heath as he ruts into me and I've never felt more protected or loved.

He angles his hips, his cock brushing against my clit

with each pass and I can feel my orgasm building and building inside of me.

"Fuck!" I cry, biting down slightly on his shoulder as I come.

Heath grits out a few curses as his pace falters and I feel him come in me a moment later. We sag against the door, both of us breathing heavy and grinning like loons.

He lets my feet slide to the floor and I wobble slightly before I find my balance.

"That was fun," Heath says, still slightly out of breath as we start to get dressed and I huff out a laugh.

"Yeah, it was," I say as I hop, tugging up my skirt and fastening the button at the back.

My phone falls out of my pocket and I tug my shirt on before I scoop it up, checking the screen to make sure that I didn't crack it.

"Oh my God," I breath as I see the missed phone calls from Charlotte's preschool.

I hit redial right away and hold my breath as I wait for the call to connect.

"Cherry Falls Preschool. This is Janet. How may I help you?"

"Hey, Janet. This is Caroline. I'm so sorry. I just saw that I had a few missed calls from you."

Heath moves closer to me, sensing my anxiety, and I know he's trying to comfort me, but I can't bring myself to look at him right now. Not until I find out why they called.

"Hey, Caroline. Yeah, we were just calling to see if you could pick Charlotte up. She and a few of her classmates have some kind of flu."

I can hear Charlotte crying in the background and my heart breaks. What kind of parent am I? I was in here screwing around with Heath when I should have been there for Charlotte.

"Yes, of course. I'll be right there," I say, already grabbing my purse and keys and pushing past Heath.

"Thanks. See you soon."

I hang up and practically sprint toward the back door and my car.

"Caroline. What can I do?" Heath asks as I climb into my car.

"Nothing. I think we've done enough," I say and I can tell that I'm close to tears.

"What? What's going on, Caroline?"

"I can't do this anymore. I can't see you anymore. I'm sorry," I say and Heath steps forward, grabbing my door before I can slam it closed.

"What? Caroline, just stop and talk to me. What is going on? You can't just end this. I love you."

My heart breaks clean down the middle at those words and at the pain and panic I see on his face.

Part of me wants to stay, to tell him what happened and let him help me take care of Charlotte, but I can't.

"I have to go," I whisper, slamming my car door and peeling out of the parking spot.

I wipe away my tears as I hurry across town to pick up Charlotte. I can't believe that I did this. I can't believe that I got so wrapped up in Heath that I didn't notice Charlotte wasn't feeling well.

It feels like I've let down my brother, sister-in-law, and Charlotte. I know that's probably not reasonable, but I can't help feeling that way. They entrusted me with their baby girl, they put me in charge of caring for her, and making sure she was safe, and I failed.

I park outside of the preschool and rush inside. My

heart breaks even more when I see Charlotte crying with her face in a trash can.

"Hey, bunny. Let's get you home," I say and she nods against my shoulder as I scoop her up in my arms and head toward the front door.

"Feel better, Charlotte!" Janet calls and I give her a tight smile as I head out to the car.

"Let me buckle you up, bunny," I say and she nods miserably.

She throws up twice on the way home and every time I look in the rearview mirror and see her tear-stained face, my decision to swear off men until she's out of the house solidifies.

I feel the final piece of my heart break as I pull into our driveway.

FOURTEEN

Heath

I WATCH CAROLINE DRIVE AWAY, wondering what the hell just happened.

Things were going so great, and then she got that call, and it all blew up in my face.

I know it has to do with Charlotte. That's the only thing that would have Caroline freaking out like that and I hope the little girl is alright.

I want to go check on them, offer to buy some Kleenex or Powerade or something, but based on how Caroline and I left things, I'm not sure I would be welcome.

I rub my chest, trying to ease the ache that's taken up root there, but it doesn't help. I can't believe I told Caroline that I loved her and she broke up with me.

I head back to my shop in a daze, not sure what to do in this situation. I close early, too heartbroken and distracted to focus on inventory or helping tourists. I'm headed to my truck when I catch sight of Dr. Coleman hurrying across the diner parking lot and assumedly back toward his clinic.

Maybe I shouldn't bother him. I know how busy he's been lately, but I need his help.

"Ken!" I call before I can stop to think it over.

He stops and looks at me in surprise.

"Hey, Heath. How's it going?"

"Alright. Hey, do you want to grab a drink with me? Do you have a few minutes?" I ask as I join him in the parking lot.

"Uh, yeah, sure. I have a few minutes."

We head down a few blocks to the Fireside Bar and Grill. It's getting to be closing time for a lot of businesses, so the bar is just starting to get crowded. We take a seat at the bar, off to the side, and I order us each a beer.

"Is everything alright, Heath? Not that I don't appreciate the beer, but you're giving off this weird kind of panicked vibe."

"Yeah, uh, no."

"What?"

"No, I'm not alright. Caroline broke up with me."

"I'm sorry to hear that," he says sympathetically.

"Things were going great, then something happened with Charlotte, and she just bolted."

Ken nods, taking a pull of his beer.

"So, I was just wondering, in your professional opinion, how do I fix this, because I can't lose her. I can't."

"You know that I'm not a psychiatrist or anything, right? And I'm single, so I'm not great with the ladies, either."

"I know, but you're the closest thing I have to a psychiatrist, and I've seen the way that Gracie looks at you, so I think you're doing alright in that other area, too."

That seems to shock him for a minute and he blinks,

frowning as he thinks that over in his head. He takes a long sip of his beer and I let him take his time as he thinks it over.

"So, what do I do now?"

"Well, we're in a bar, so if you want to move on or find someone else then—"

I don't let him finish his sentence.

"No. There is no one else for me," I say, my voice coming out harsher than I intended. "There's no one else. I just want Caroline."

He nods like he expected that and I pick at the label on my beer bottle.

"Then let her come to the same conclusion."

"What if she doesn't?" I ask, voicing the one thought I can't escape.

"She will," he says simply.

"But how can I make her see it faster?"

I've wasted months trying to get her to warm up to me, trying to work up the nerve to ask her out and now that I've had the real thing, I can't go back to the way it was before.

"So, you think this breakup has to do with Charlotte?"

"Yeah, she was acting a little off yesterday and this morning and I think maybe she's sick or something. At first, we just thought that she was tired from her sleepover, but I don't know. The only thing that can freak out Caroline is something happening to Charlotte."

"Yeah, she and a few other parents have been bringing their kids in to see me this afternoon. Some kind of bug is going around."

"Is Charlotte okay?" I ask, alarmed.

What if it's serious and I haven't been there for them?

"I can't tell you any specific details, but it's nothing serious, and I'm sure all of the kids will be back to normal soon."

"Good," I say, relieved that Charlotte will be back to feeling better soon.

"Is this the first time Charlotte has been sick while Caroline was caring for her?"

"I think it might be. She's only been her guardian for a little while."

"That has to be pretty overwhelming. I'm sure that being a single mom is hard and stressful. Maybe she just overreacted or panicked. Maybe she just needs to see that you're not going to abandon her when the going gets tough."

I mull over his words. Could he have a point? Maybe Caroline was just upset that she wasn't there for Charlotte, or maybe she thought I would distract her from taking care of her.

"So, what do I do?"

"Talk to her and find out what upset her. If it is about Charlotte, then try to show her that you're not going anywhere. That you don't want to distract her from being the best mom to Charlotte. That you just want to help and be a part of their lives."

He's right. I told Caroline that I loved her, but maybe's it time I show her that I do. I need to show her I'm not going anywhere and I won't give up or stop fighting for us.

I'm going to fix this.

"Thanks, Ken."

"Anytime."

I throw some cash onto the bar, nodding to the bartender as I head out to my truck. Part of me, a really big part, wants to head over to Caroline's place right now, but I don't want to wake up Charlotte or Caroline if they're resting.

Starting tomorrow, though, I'm winning back my girls.

FIFTEEN

Caroline

I'M JUST CLEANING up and trying to disinfect every square inch of our house when there's a knock on the door. Gracie is supposed to be dropping off a few things for Charlotte so I don't think anything of it when I open the door.

My stomach drops when I see Heath standing there, two brown paper bags clutched in his hands.

"Hey," he says, his eyes drinking me in greedily.

I'm sure that I look like a mess. I've been up for almost twenty-four hours with Charlotte. She keeps throwing up and I was so worried about her that I didn't sleep last night. I just sat next to her bed to make sure she was alright.

I'm still in my pajamas, my hair tangled and twisted on top of my head in a messy ponytail. My hands are full of Clorox wipes and Lysol spray and I shift them to one hand.

"Hey," I say, self-consciously reaching up to try to fix my messy ponytail.

"How's Charlotte doing?"

"Um, about the same. She's sleeping right now," I tell him.

"I uh, I ran into Gracie and she said she was bringing this stuff over to you, so I volunteered. She was busy with some order at the flower shop."

"Thanks," I say, setting the cleaning supplies on the table by the door and reaching for the bags.

"Let me put them in the kitchen for you."

Heath pushes past me and heads for the kitchen. I frown and follow after him.

"Thanks for bringing these by."

"Of course."

"You should leave before you catch what Charlotte has."

"I need to talk to you," he says, leaning against the kitchen counter and eyeing me.

"No, you don't."

It's hard enough being in the same room as him. I just want to go to him, to lay my head against his strong chest and let him hold me, let him help me with Charlotte and cleaning up. I can't, though. I need to take care of Charlotte. She has to be my sole focus right now.

"Yes, I do," he insists and I cross my arms.

"There's nothing to talk about."

"Caroline, I love you. I'm not going anywhere until you tell me why you got so scared yesterday and dumped me out of the blue."

"Maybe I just wasn't feeling it anymore," I lie.

"Doubt it, considering I was inside of you, like, thirty seconds prior."

My face flames as I think about the way he took me against my office door.

"Maybe that was just goodbye."

He doesn't have an answer for that but I can see the flash of pain in his eyes at my words. I can't handle that. I don't want to hurt him. Heath has been nothing but good and kind to me and it's not fair of me to cause him pain now.

"I need to think about Charlotte right now. She's my responsibility. I'm all the family she has left and she needs to be my top priority right now."

Heath studies me for a moment, scrutinizing me.

"That's just an excuse."

"No, it's not," I say, growing defensive.

"I never wanted to make you choose between Charlotte and me. Even if I did, I would expect you to choose her every time. I just wanted to be a part of your life. I just wanted to be with you."

"Aunt Caroline?" Charlotte calls and she sounds so weak and miserable that my stomach clenches.

"I can't do this right now. I have to go."

Heath nods, seeming disappointed as he turns to go.

"I'll wait for you, Caroline. You're the only girl that I've ever wanted and soon Charlotte is going to get better and you're going to realize we were meant to be. Then you'll come back to me."

I just stare at him as he steps over the threshold. His gaze holds mine and then he leans down, brushing a kiss against my cheek.

"I'll wait for you," he whispers again against my ear and I can't stop the shiver that skates down my spine.

I want to go to him now. I want to admit that I made a mistake, that I panicked and that I need him, but Charlotte calls for me again and I step back inside.

"Bye, Heath. Thanks for the groceries."

He nods and I close the front door, leaning back against it for a minute as I try to ease the ache in my chest.

"Aunt Caroline?" Charlotte asks as she stops at the top of the stairs and I force a smile.

"I'm coming, bunny," I say as I push away from the door and head upstairs to take care of her.

SIXTEEN

Heath

IT'S BEEN a week of nothing.

No texts or calls from Caroline.

No lunches.

Not even a sighting of her beautiful face.

I'm not sure how much longer I can go on like this.

I've still been going to the diner every day for lunch, but she hasn't been in. Charlotte is still recovering and so she's staying home with her.

If she comes in to work in the morning or later at night to take care of stuff, I don't see her. And I've been looking. I find myself staring out the front window of my shop, obsessively watching the diner to see if I can catch just a glimpse of her.

"Dude, you're like, leering," Graham says as he leans against the front counter.

He's back in town to pick up the last of his supplies before winter hits up in Fallen Peak and I was supposed to be ringing him up, but I thought that I saw Caroline and Charlotte. I've been staring across the street at the diner for a few minutes, hoping I catch another sight of them.

"Sorry, I uh, I've been a little distracted lately," I admit.

"This about your girl?"

"Yeah. Her niece is sick with the flu and I haven't seen them in a few days."

"Hope she feels better soon."

"Thanks. Me too."

We're silent as I start to ring him up.

"That's not what's bothering you, though," Graham says and I wonder how he always does that.

It's like the guy can read minds or something. Or maybe I'm just an open book.

"No. She broke up with me last week. Said that her niece has to be her main priority."

"Well, that makes sense. You can't be mad at her for that."

"I'm not. I'm not mad at her at all."

"You just want her back," he states and I nod.

"Yeah. I need her."

Graham nods.

"Have you tried to talk to her?"

"Yeah, I told her that I'd wait for her. That I knew that she was going to come back to me because she knew how good we are together."

"Okay then, just give her some time."

"Easier said than done."

Graham gives me a grim smile as I finish ringing up his purchases.

"Good luck with your lady. If I can do anything or be there for you, just let me know, man."

"Thanks, Graham."

"Sure," he says, nodding his head and I can tell that he doesn't really know how to help me or be there for me right now.

"I can't wait until the day that you fall head over heels for someone and come to me for advice."

"Never going to happen, man, Graham says with a laugh and I smile.

"We'll see."

I help him load up his truck and wave as he heads back up to Fallen Peak. Once his truck is out of sight, I turn back to the diner, my eyes hungrily scanning for a glimpse of Caroline and Charlotte, but I don't see them or her car in the lot.

I sigh, turning and heading back inside. Looks like I'm in for another lonely night.

SEVENTEEN

Caroline

"SO, I think it must be what Charlotte had last week. I've been nauseous and tired," I tell Dr. Coleman and he nods, writing something down in my chart.

"Let's check you out."

I shift on the exam table, the thin paper crinkling under my legs.

"Any fever in the last few days?"

"No," I admit and he frowns.

"Hmm."

He checks my temperature, blood pressure, looks in my eyes and ears and feels my lymph nodes.

"Are you feeling nauseous right now?" he asks.

"No, it's more in the afternoons," I admit.

He writes something else down and then takes a seat next to the table.

"Any other symptoms?"

"Just feel kind of emotional and tired."

"Okay."

I watch him as he writes down something else.

"Well, without the fever and the all-day nauseousness, it doesn't sound like it's the bug that's going around that Charlotte had."

"Okay," I say, starting to get a little nervous.

"Are you under a lot of stress?"

My mind flashes to how awful this last week has been. Between getting Charlotte back to feeling one hundred percent and nursing my own broken heart, I haven't been eating or sleeping as much as I should.

I thought maybe that's what this was initially, but now that I've started throwing up, I just wanted to see Dr. Coleman to make sure.

"I guess a little. I wasn't eating or sleeping great while I was caring for Charlotte."

He nods, thinking something over.

"I uh, I heard about you and Heath."

My stomach cramps and I squirm slightly. The paper crinkles, the only sound in the room.

"Yeah..."

"Do you think maybe that could be causing some of the symptoms?" he asks gently and I shrug.

"Does that actually make people sick?" I ask.

"Sure, the stress and emotional distress from a breakup can cause problems or health concerns."

I bite my bottom lip, mulling that over. I have been pretty upset about the break up and between that and Charlotte being sick, I haven't been taking care of myself.

"There's one other possibility," Dr. Coleman says and I nod. "You could be pregnant."

My stomach drops and I try to think back to when my last period was.

I can't believe I never even thought about using protection with Heath. Or that he never brought it up, either. Wasn't he worried about this happening?

"Do you remember when your last menstrual cycle was?"

"Um," I try to think back to the date but draw a blank.

"Well, let's do a pregnancy test just to be safe. If it comes back as negative then we can try to run some more tests."

I nod, my hands clammy as I twist my fingers together in my lap.

I follow Dr. Coleman up front and he hands me a cup and points me toward the bathroom with a gentle smile.

My hands shake as I do the test and I leave it in the designated spot.

"I'll call you later today with the results," Dr. Coleman says and I nod as I grab my purse and head outside to my car.

It's almost time for me to go pick up Charlotte, so I head toward her preschool, my mind in a daze as I think about the possibility of being pregnant.

I'm going to have to tell Heath.

I park and smile when I see Charlotte playing outside on the playground. She spots me and waves, running over to the fence, so I climb out and head over to meet her.

"Hey, bunny!" I greet her and she grins at me.

"Are we going to the diner?" she asks excitedly and I smile.

Her appetite has come back and she's been devouring the vegetable soup and grilled cheese that David makes for her.

"Sure. Let me just check you out."

She nods and runs back to her friends and I head inside to tell Janet that I'm picking Charlotte up.

"See you on Monday!" she says and I smile and wave.

I load Charlotte into her car seat and she tells me all about her day as we make the short drive over to the Virgin Street Diner.

"Can we go camping this weekend? We haven't seen Heath in so long," she says, drawing out the *so long*.

I haven't told her yet that we broke up, and I don't want to think about why. At first I told myself it was just because she was sick and I didn't want to cause her more stress, but then she got better and I still didn't tell her.

Part of me knows it's because I don't really want it to be over.

"Um, maybe," I stall and she huffs out a sigh.

"I miss him," she says quietly and I nod, my eyes starting to water.

"Me too," I admit.

We head inside and I get Charlotte settled in a booth and go to grab her a chocolate milk and place her order.

My eyes stray to the front windows and I look across the street to the Cherry Falls Trading Post. I can see Heath behind the counter and he looks up, meeting my eyes for a brief second.

That's it. That one look and I know I can't go on like this.

He looks as miserable as I feel and I can't take it. I can't stand not seeing him for another second.

"Hey, Gracie?" I ask as she eats her food at the counter.

"Yeah?"

"Can you watch Charlotte for just a second?"

"Sure!" she says, grabbing her drink and plate and heading over to the booth.

I watch them sit together for a minute before I take a deep breath and head for the front door. I make it across the street and open the door, almost running into Heath as I walk inside.

"Hey," I say as he reaches out and steadies me.

"Hey," he says, eyeing me hopefully.

"I'm so sorry," I choke out and the next thing I know, Heath's lips are on mine.

He kisses me hard, our hands clinging to each other's clothes as we try to get as close as possible to each other. He pulls away just as abruptly as he started the kiss and I'm left feeling off balance.

"Thank fuck. I was losing my mind without you," he breathes as he rests his forehead against mine.

"Me too," I admit. "I'm sorry that I panicked and pushed you away. I need you. I love you, too. So much."

He kisses me again, his tongue slipping into my open mouth and I tug on the short strands of his hair, loving how he makes me feel, how perfect we are together.

"I love you," he says as his lips land back on mine.

"Uh huh," I mumble, kissing him back.

"I missed you so much."

"I have something else that I should tell you," I say as we come up for air.

"What's that?" he asks, tugging me closer to his body.

"I went to see Dr. Coleman today because I wasn't feeling well the last few days, and I wanted to make sure I didn't have what Charlotte had."

Heath's brow wrinkles and I can see the worry in his eyes. His hands tighten on my waist, like holding me closer is going to cure me of whatever ailment I might have.

"Is it the flu? Should you be up? I can watch Charlotte if you need to rest."

"No, it's not the flu. He said, well, he said I might be pregnant."

Heath freezes, his eyes dropping to my stomach and I bite my bottom lip.

"Really?" he whispers, his voice filled with awe.

"Maybe," I stress and he drops to his knees in front of me.

"Is it wrong that I hope you are?"

"No," I say as he kisses my stomach, a smile on his lips.

"I love you, Caroline, and whether you are or not, I want to be with you. Forever."

"I love you, too, and I want to be with you forever, too."

He kisses my stomach one more time before he stands and tucks me under his arm.

"Let's go see Charlotte," he says, and I smile, letting him lead me back across the street to the diner.

EIGHTEEN

Heath

ONE YEAR LATER...

"I'LL GRAB THAT," I tell Caroline but she just rolls her eyes, grabbing the bag of chips and heading into the cabin.

I might be going a little overboard, but she's so far along now and I get worried about her overdoing things.

Turns out, she wasn't pregnant when we got back together. It had just been stress throwing off her cycle, but we found out that we were expecting five months later.

By then, we were married and had moved in together. I moved into their place since we didn't want to disrupt Charlotte's routine too much.

Charlotte was Caroline's maid of honor at the wedding and she got to walk down the aisle with her pet bunny, Mudslide. I had caved and bought her one for her fifth birthday. The thing is cute and loves Charlotte.

"Rooney, can you grab the cooler?" Sayler calls to her husband.

We're all up at my cabin for the weekend. I've met Caroline's friends a few times now. We went up to Pittsburgh for Sayler's and Coraline's weddings, and they came to Cherry Falls for ours. This is the first trip we've taken with them, though, and I'm a little nervous.

I actually like Rooney and Harvey, but I'm also a little terrified of Rooney. The guy is wild, and while he's hilarious and a good time to hang out with, he's also clumsy.

I follow my wife inside, making sure that Charlotte is okay playing with the dogs and Mudslide.

"Having fun?" I ask as I crouch down to see what she's coloring.

"Yeah. Are we going to make s'mores soon?"

"Sure, we can do that right after we eat dinner. Are you hungry?"

She nods, going back to coloring the picture of Caroline, me, Mudslide, and her in front of our house. I kiss her head before I start to stand.

"Maybe we should start a fire?" Sayler calls and I move to head out back to do it when I hear Rooney yell.

"I'll get it going."

"Oh my God, no!" I shout, running through the kitchen and out the back door.

I can hear my wife and her friends laughing but I'm dead serious. Rooney is liable to set himself or the cabin on fire before he gets it going.

"I'll get it," I tell Rooney and he shrugs, but I can see the grin. He likes scaring the crap out of me.

"Food's almost done!" Coraline calls, and he and Harvey head inside as I stack the logs to start the campfire.

It's getting dark and I know we'll probably eat out here

since there isn't enough chairs or room inside. If these camping trips become a regular thing, we're going to have to buy a new cabin or build onto this one.

"I made you a plate," Caroline says as she comes outside and I kiss her, taking the plate and smiling as Charlotte takes the chair next to me.

"S'mores," Charlotte whispers as she shoves a huge bite of hot dog into her mouth and I laugh.

"Soon," I promise her and she smiles.

Charlotte and I have grown closer over the last year. She loves to be outdoors, so I try to pick her up from school at least twice a week so that we can go hiking or sledding in the winter. I think she likes that she gets time alone with me and I like that I get to share something special with her.

Caroline takes a seat on my other side and I smile, passing her the water bottle I grabbed for her earlier.

"Thanks."

She leans over and kisses my cheek and I finish my food, leaving her the chips that I know she's been craving lately.

"You're the best," she says when I put them on her plate and I laugh.

I rub her neck as she eats and look around at our friends. I was always a bit of a loner, but now I have friends, a daughter, and another kid on the way, as well as the woman of my dreams. I have this whole family and it's more than I could have ever hoped for, but it's exactly what I need.

"Ready for s'mores?" I ask, and I can't help but laugh when Rooney and Charlotte both shout yes.

Life with my girls is perfect.

NINETEEN

Caroline

TEN YEARS LATER…

"READY FOR DATE NIGHT?" I ask Heath as I come into the bathroom where he's brushing his teeth and he nods enthusiastically, causing me to laugh.

"Me, too. It's been too long," I say as I tie my hair up on top of my head.

I'm already dressed and we need to drop the kids off at Gracie and Ken's place in a few minutes so they can babysit for us. Our kids are best friends with theirs, so it's really more like a play date. We take turns, switching off every other month so that we each get a bit of a break and some alone time with our husbands.

Heath and I have been married for ten years now and have three wonderful kids. Charlotte loves being the big sister and she's so patient with Calvin and Rhys.

"Come on, Mom and Dad!" Rhys yells from downstairs and I grin at Heath in the mirror.

"Ready?" he asks and I nod, letting him take my hand and lead me downstairs.

The kids talk excitedly about what they're going to do over at the Coleman's. Some new movie just came out and they can't wait to watch it. They practically jump out of the car before we've even parked and I laugh as I walk them up to the front door.

"Hey guys!" Gracie says as she opens the door and the kids yell *hi* as they dart past her to catch up with their friends.

"Hey," I say and she laughs.

"The kids are jumping on the trampoline now that it's not a hundred degrees out."

"They've been talking about coming over all day. Thanks so much for watching them."

"Of course! You two have fun. We'll see you in a few hours."

I wave and head back down the path to our car. Heath got out to open my door for me and I drop a kiss on his lips as he helps me up into the passenger seat.

"Where are we going?" I ask him.

We take turns planning our dates, and this month is his turn. I'm excited to see what he has set up for us.

"It's a surprise," he says as he laces our fingers together and I rest back against the seat and let him drive.

We talk about our businesses on the drive. Both are doing good and this last year we've been talking about expanding. Maybe open a diner in the next town over or something. Heath had mentioned opening a place up in Fallen Peak so he can see his friend Graham more. He knows I get along with Graham's wife and the kids have fun playing with each other, too, but it's quite a drive.

"Ready?" Heath asks as he parks outside of our cabin.

We've had to add onto it twice now as our family grows, but it's perfect and the kids love coming up here for long weekends to camp.

I let Heath lead me inside and I grin when I see the tent set up in the living room.

"Just like that first night," I say and he grins at me.

"Yeah, but now I can do all of the things that I wanted to do to you back then."

"Oh, is that so? Are there a lot of things?" I ask as he leads me over to the tent.

"So many."

I giggle as he kisses my neck and I look around the place. There's a campfire nightlight going in the fireplace since it's too hot to light a real fire and string lights zig zag over the ceiling, making it look like stars.

"I love it. Thank you for doing all of this for tonight."

"I'd do anything for you, Caroline. You know that."

He's right. I do. He's been the best husband, the best dad to all of our kids. He's so patient and he always makes time for each of them so that no one feels left out.

I duck inside the tent and smile as I see the mountain of pillows and the sleeping bags lying on the floor. There's some snacks and drinks in a corner and an iPad next to it.

"Are we watching a movie?" I ask him as I lay back on the pillows.

"If you want."

"I want to do something else," I say, grabbing his shirt collar and pulling him closer to me.

"Yeah?"

"Yeah," I whisper a second before our lips meet.

I wiggle out of my maxi dress and Heath pulls away to stare hungrily down my body.

"Perfect," he whispers in awe and I love that even after all of these years he still can't get enough of me.

"I love you," I tell him and his eyes meet mine.

"I love you, too."

He spends the next few hours showing me just how much.

DID you love 803 Wishing Lane? Please consider leaving a review! You can do so on Amazon or on Goodreads!

DYING to learn how Gracie and Ken got their happily ever after? Check out 1012 Curvy Way! You can read it here.

WANT to learn more about Harvey or Rooney? Check out the Eye Candy Ink: Second Generation series here.

Want to learn more about Graham and the other mountain men of Fallen Peak? Check out the series here.

ALSO BY SHAW HART

· · ·

STILL IN THE **mood for Christmas books?**

Stuffing Her Stocking, Mistletoe Kisses, Snowed in For Christmas

LOVE HOLIDAY BOOKS? **Check out these!**

For Better or Worse, Riding His Broomstick, Thankful for His FAKE Girlfriend, His New Year Resolution, Hop Stuff, Taming Her Beast, Hungry For Dash, His Firework

LOOKING **for some OTT love stories?**

Fighting for His Princess, Her Scottish Savior, Not So Accidental Baby Daddy, Baby Mama

LOOKING FOR A CELEBRITY LOVE STORY?

Bedroom Eyes, Seducing Archer, Finding Their Rhythm

IN THE MOOD **for some young love books?**

Study Dates, His Forever, My Girl

SOME OTHER BOOKS BY SHAW:

The Billionaire's Bet, Her Guardian Angel, Every Tuesday Night, Falling Again, Stealing Her, Dreamboat, Locked Down, Making Her His, Trouble

CONNECT WITH ME!

If you enjoyed this story, please consider leaving a review on Amazon or any other reader site or blog that you like. Don't forget to recommend it to your other reader friends.

If you want to chat with me, please consider joining my VIP list or connecting with me on one of my Social Media platforms. I love talking with each of my readers. Links below!

Website
Newsletter

Claiming His Forever

Finding His Forever

Rescuing His Forever

Chasing His Forever

Folklore: The Complete Series

Wish Series:

His Wish

Her Wish

Obsessed Series:

Her Obsession

His Obsession

Mine To Series:

Mine to Love

Mine to Protect

Mine to Cherish

Mine to Keep